Super DC Heroes Villains

Cheetah and the Purrfect Crime

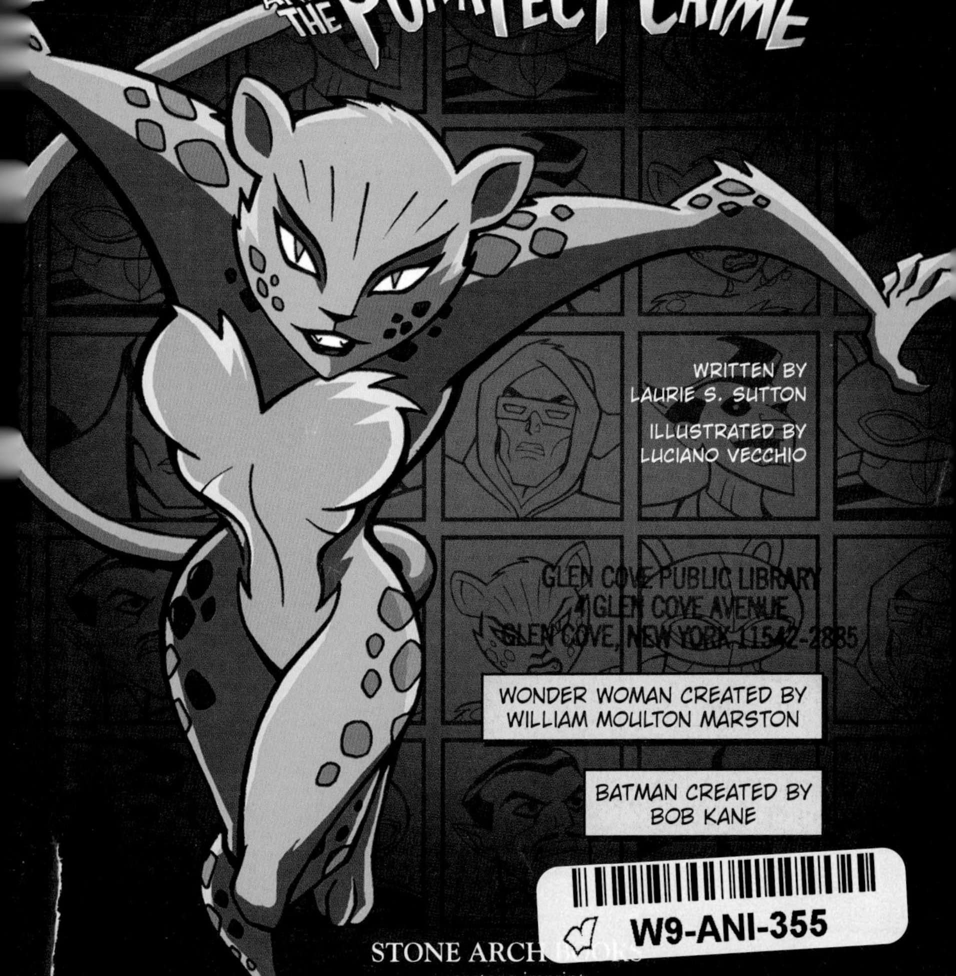

Written by Laurie S. Sutton

Illustrated by Luciano Vecchio

Wonder Woman created by William Moulton Marston

Batman created by Bob Kane

Stone Arch Books
a capstone imprint

Published by Stone Arch Books in 2012
A Capstone Imprint
1710 Roe Crest Drive
North Mankato, MN 56003
www.capstonepub.com

STAR25085

Cataloging-in-Publication Data is available at
the Library of Congress website

ISBN: 978-1-4342-3799-6 (library binding)
ISBN: 978-1-4342-3900-6 (paperback)

Summary: A cat burglar is on the loose in
Gotham City! Batman suspects the evil
Catwoman, but this crime spree is too
purrfect for one kitty crook. With the help of
Wonder Woman, the World's Greatest Detective
picks up the paw prints of another feline felon,
the quick and crafty super-villain, Cheetah.

Printed in the United States of America in Stevens Point,
Wisconsin.
102011
006404WZS12

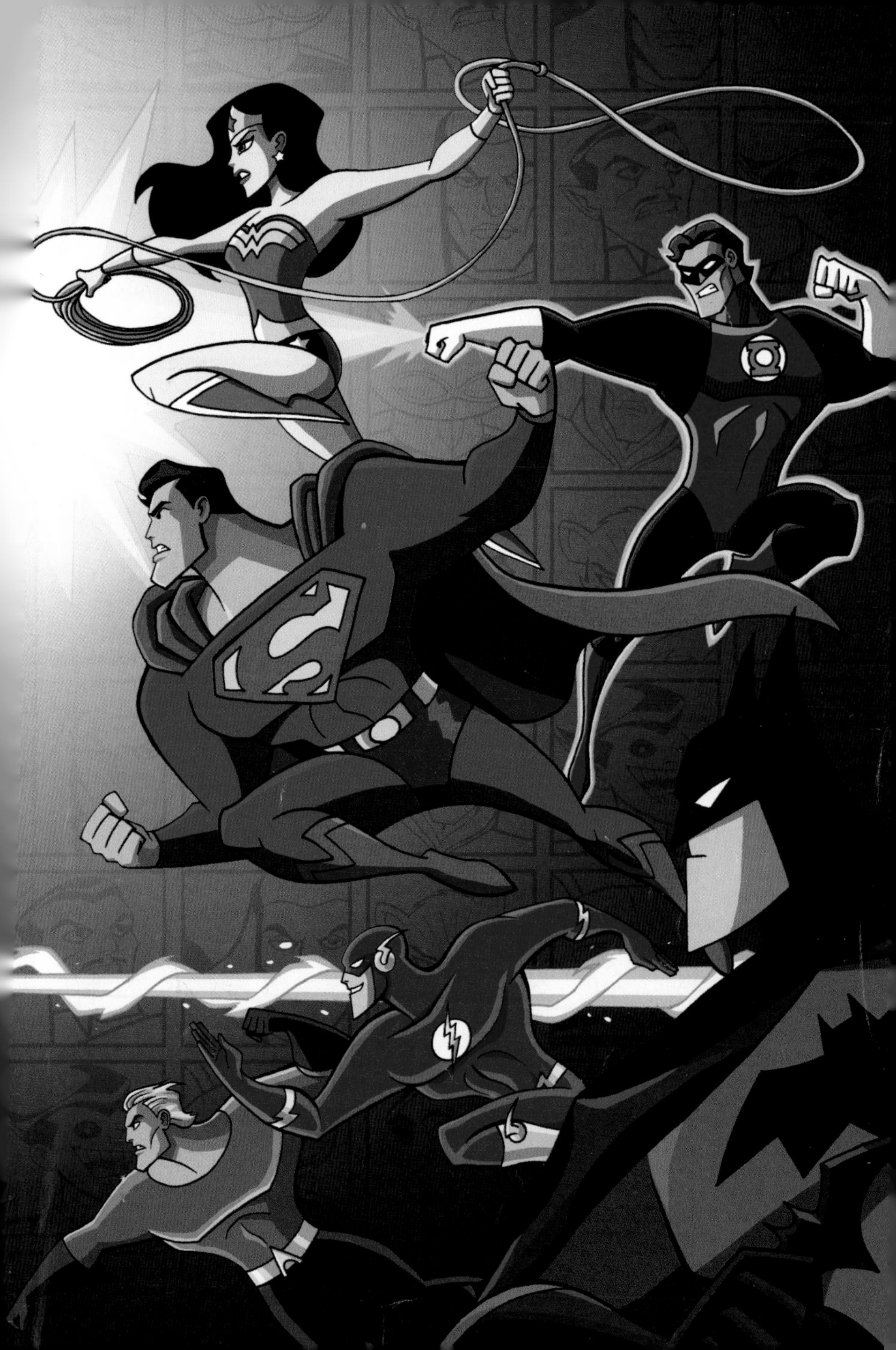

TABLE OF CONTENTS

CHEETAH

REAL NAME:
Barbara Ann Minerva

OCCUPATION: Biologist

HEIGHT: 5' 9"

WEIGHT: 120 lbs.

EYES: Brown

HAIR: Auburn

BIOGRAPHY:

Dr. Barbara Ann Minerva was a successful biologist who was working on ground-breaking genetics research. Her tests, however, were very expensive. She ran out of money to fund them. Desperate to finish her studies, Dr. Minerva tested her highly experimental research on herself. As a result, her body was transformed into a half-human, half-cheetah hybrid. Shunned by the scientific community, and seen as a freak by the rest of the world, Cheetah has turned to crime to fund her efforts to once again become human.

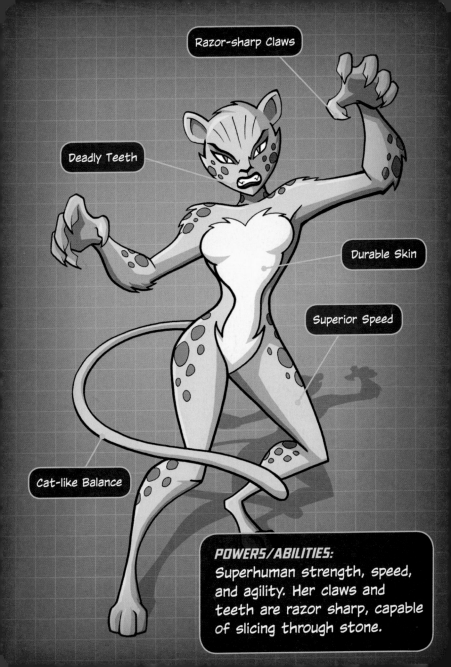

Razor-sharp Claws

Deadly Teeth

Durable Skin

Superior Speed

Cat-like Balance

POWERS/ABILITIES:
Superhuman strength, speed,
and agility. Her claws and
teeth are razor sharp, capable
of slicing through stone.

CHAPTER 1

IDENTITY THEFT

It was midnight, but Cheetah's day was just getting started. The super-villain stood atop the tallest building in Gotham. She had a spectacular view of the city lights below and the stars above. But none of that mattered to her — Cheetah was interested in only one thing.

"I need money, Gotham," Cheetah growled. "And you're my new bank. Consider this plan my first withdrawal."

Cheetah was visiting Gotham City and didn't know much about the town.

That fact wasn't important. All she really needed to know was that there were places to rob and valuables to steal.

Still, there was one thing everybody knew about Gotham City. It was the home of the World's Greatest Detective, Batman. Cheetah didn't want to get caught, so she had a plan to stay out of his sights.

"Batman will never know I'm the one behind the crimes," Cheetah said with an evil laugh. "Not if he thinks they're Catwoman's fault!" Cheetah pulled a costume out of a paper shopping bag. It looked exactly like the uniform of another super-villain known as Catwoman.

She put on the hood, and then pulled on the rest of the skin-tight suit. "Grrrr. How does Catwoman wear this?" Cheetah complained, wriggling into the costume.

Cheetah wiggled and stomped to get the costume up to her hips. Then she stopped. Her tail wouldn't fit!

Cheetah used one of her sharp claws to tear a hole in the costume. Now her tail fit through the suit. Then she pulled the rest of the costume over her body, and poked her claws through the black leather gloves.

"I'm dressed for the part," Cheetah said. "Now I can commit any cat crime and blame it on Catwoman."

WHOOOOSH!

Cheetah leaped off the building. She had picked her target — a Gotham jewelry store. Diamond bracelets and necklaces glittered in the window. They were made in the shapes of tigers and leopards.

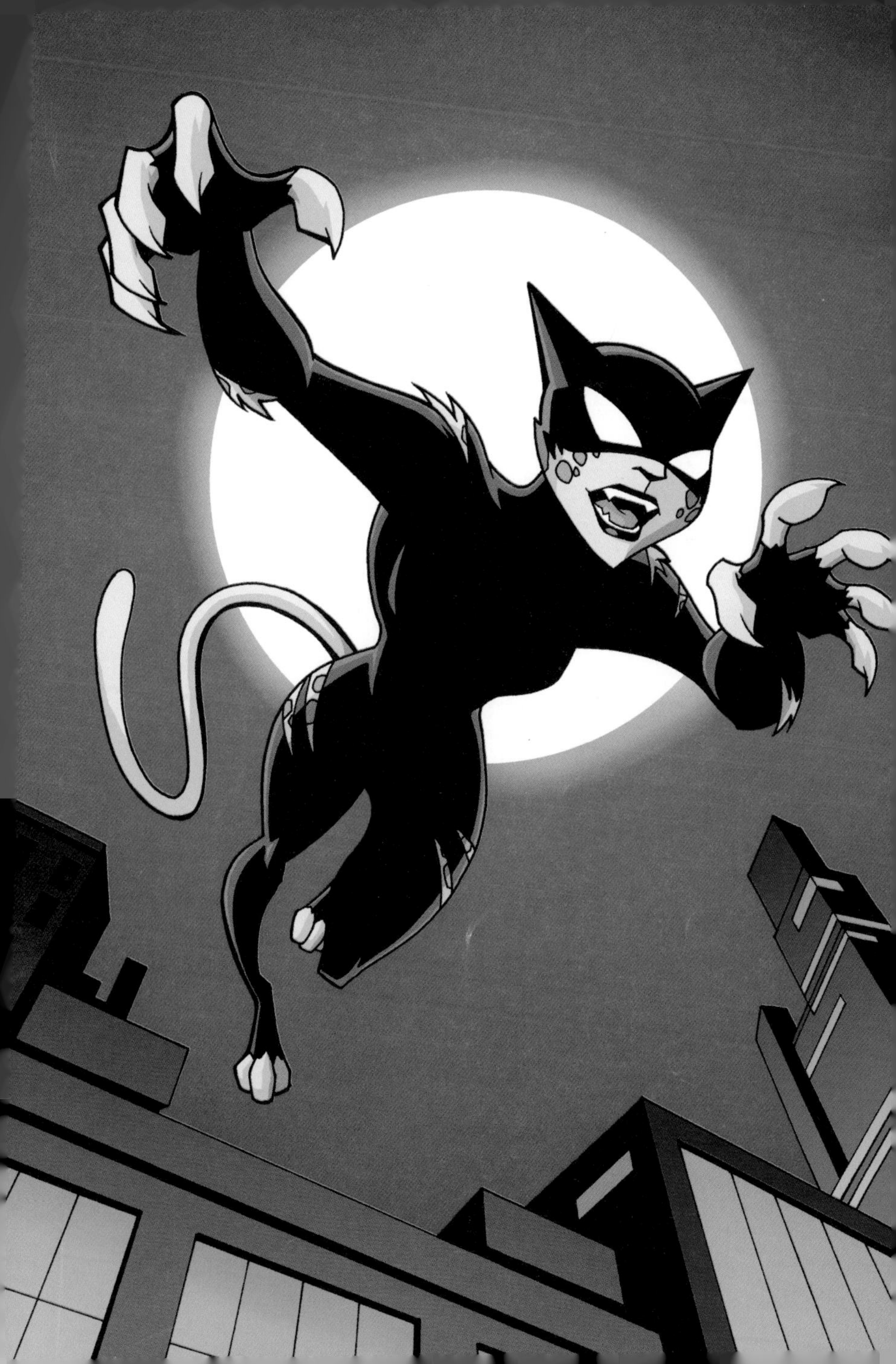

"Meow! Catwoman wants those pretty kitties," Cheetah joked, imitating the voice of her fellow feline felon.

Cheetah used one of her razor-sharp claws to cut a hole in the store's glass window. It was bulletproof, but it wasn't Cheetah-proof. She reached into the display and grabbed a leopard necklace.

BEEP! BEEP! BEEP!

The burglar alarm suddenly went off.

"Uh-oh," Cheetah exclaimed. "Time for this cat to scat!"

The super-villain snatched another cat-shaped necklace and darted down an alley. Just like the animal that shared her name, Cheetah was very, very fast. She was ten blocks away before police officers arrived at the jewelry store.

Meanwhile, Cheetah's crime spree continued. The Gotham Gallery of Art was exhibiting rare Aztec jaguar statues. The sculptures were hundreds of years old, which made them extremely valuable to art collectors. They were also made of solid gold, and that made them worth stealing!

Cheetah slipped into the art gallery through an air vent in the roof. The super-villain crawled along the rafters on all fours like a cat. *SNIFF! SNIFF!* Cheetah cautiously sniffed the air and caught the scent of something stinky.

The museum's night guard was singing a song to pass the time. The sound was terrible to Cheetah's ears. She pulled back into the shadows. She didn't want to be seen by whatever monster was making this noise.

The guard tried to reach the high notes but failed.

Cheetah was relieved that she didn't have anything to fear, but she was angry that she had felt fear at all.

"Roaaarrr!" Cheetah snarled and dropped from the rafters.

The night guard fell under Cheetah's assault. He never expected an attack. He worked the night shift because it was supposed to be quiet.

SLAAASH! Cheetah flashed her claws. She did not think. She was all animal. She stopped only when her prey didn't move anymore, unconscious.

"That's the difference between us," a female voice interrupted. "You're the wild cat, and I'm the clever cat."

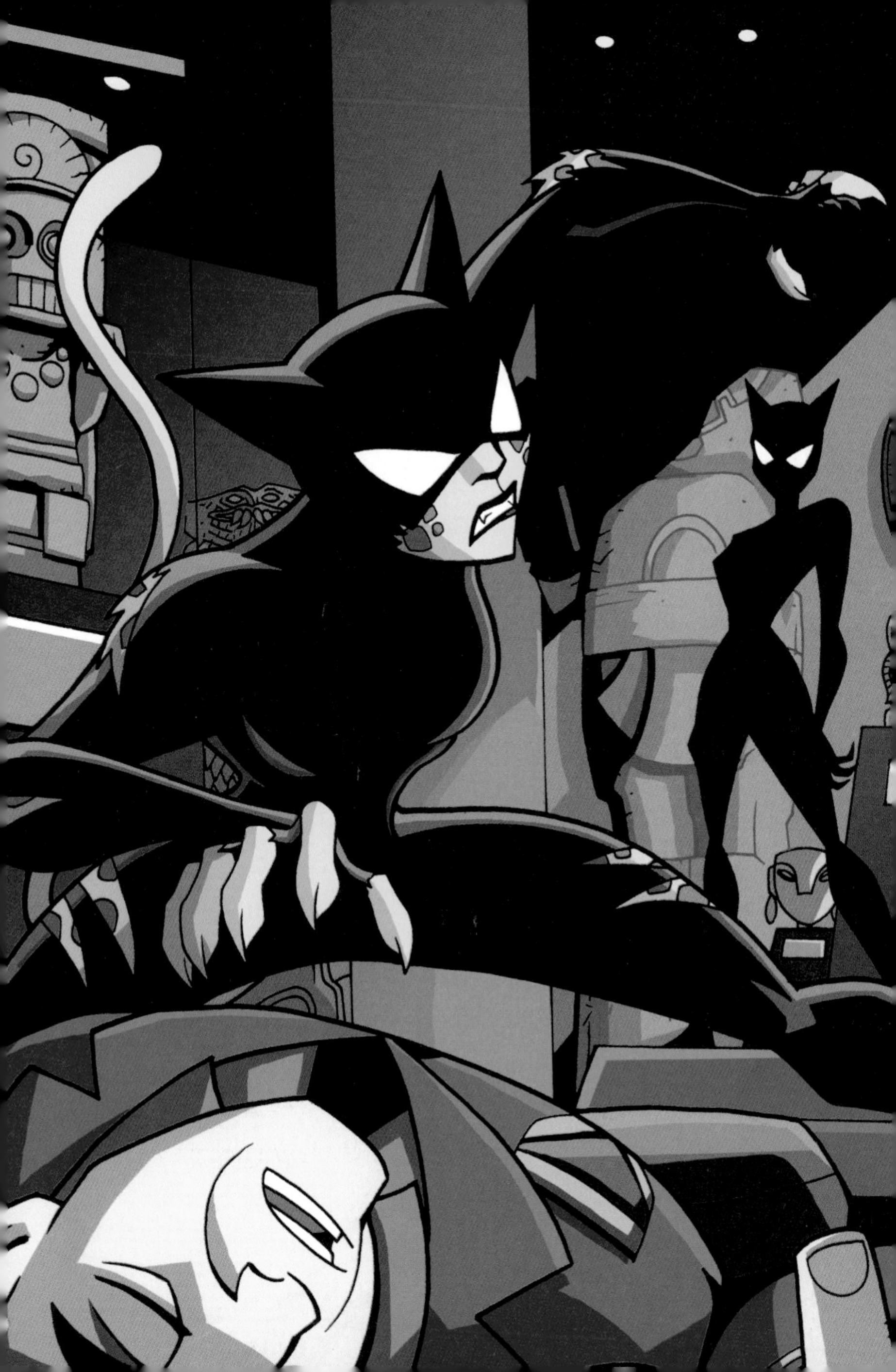

Cheetah's mind was still muddled from the heart-pumping action of her attack. She struggled to regain her senses. A slim female figure took form in front of her eyes as they regained focus.

"Who are you?" Cheetah demanded.

Sharp metal fingernails grabbed Cheetah by her Catwoman costume. The fabric split, and the suit ripped from Cheetah's body.

"Who am I?" the figure mocked. "You should know! You're pretending to be me!"

Cheetah finally recognized the person in front of her. "Oh," she said. "Hello, Catwoman."

CHAPTER 2

PARTNERS IN CRIME

"You know, they say that imitation is the highest form of flattery," Catwoman said. She looked down at the ripped Catwoman costume. "But I'm not feeling very flattered."

"I didn't come to Gotham to flatter you," Cheetah hissed. "I came for the easy loot."

Cheetah reached for the gold jaguar statue, but Catwoman grabbed her wrist.

"Not so fast!" Catwoman said. "You'll set off the alarms. Are you always so careless?"

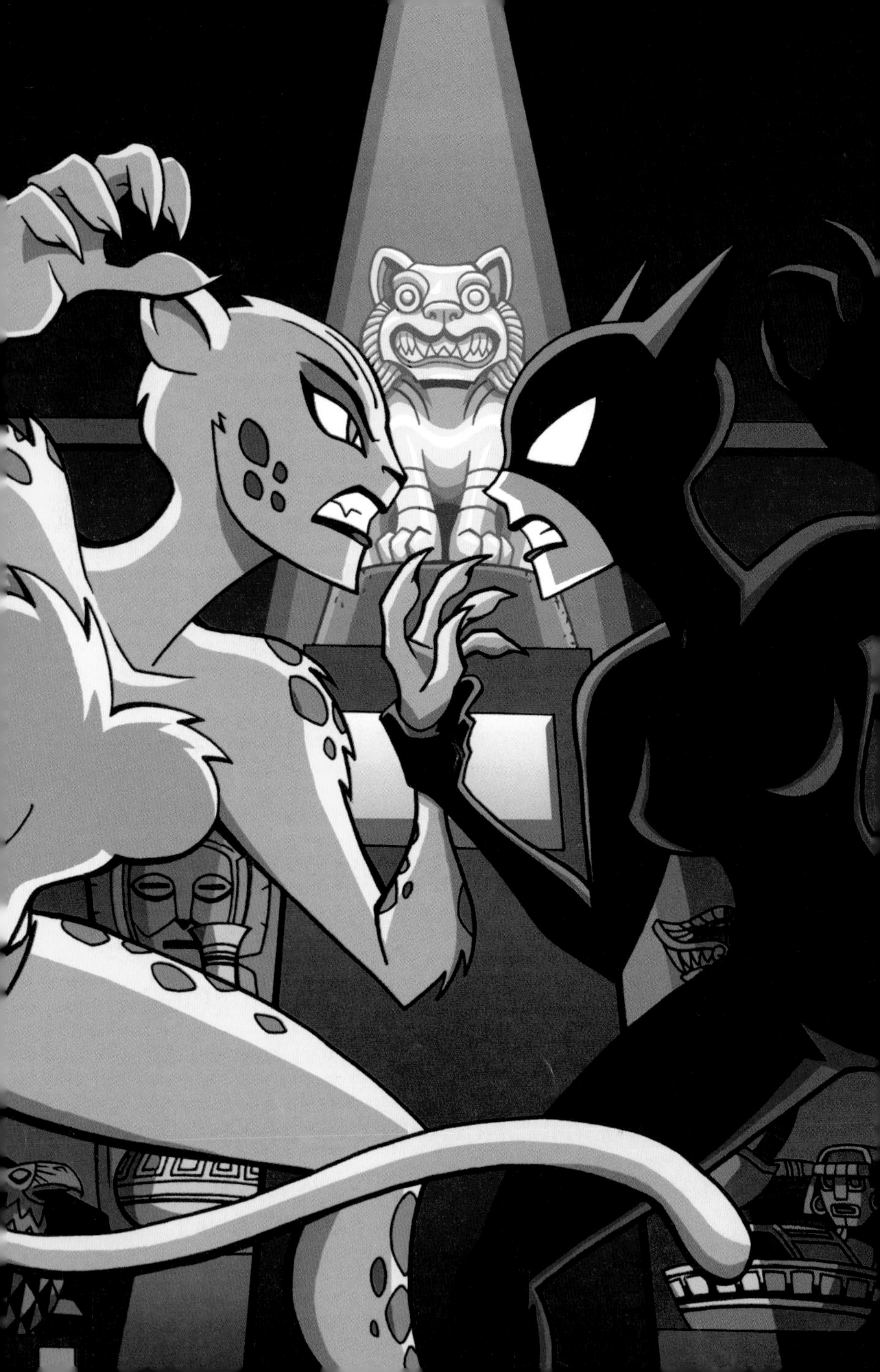

Hisssssss Cheetah bared her fangs at the comment. She felt insulted. She pulled her wrist from Catwoman's grasp, but didn't make a move toward the statue.

"Obviously you dressed like me so it will look like I've stolen this statue," Catwoman said. "Which I plan to do, by the way."

"I was here first!" Cheetah shouted.

The two cat crooks stared into each other's eyes. Neither wanted to back down.

"Wait!" Catwoman said before Cheetah grabbed the statue and set off the alarms. "I have a plan that will help both of us!"

"What sort of plan?" Cheetah asked.

"We should team up," Catwoman suggested. "You can keep committing cat crimes. I'll do the same. The police will never know they're tracking two cats."

Cheetah considered the plan.

"Come on. It'll be a lovely game of cat-and-mouse — or, should I say, cat-and-cat!" Catwoman added.

"All right," Cheetah agreed. "But I get this statue!" Cheetah used her super-fast reflexes to grab the golden jaguar.

BEEP! BEEP! BEEP!

Alarms blared. Both felines laughed as they ran from the art gallery.

Cheetah and Catwoman scampered up to the rafters and out the air vent. They heard police sirens coming toward the gallery. Cheetah's sharp eyes spotted the patrol cars. She pointed them out to Catwoman.

"Thanks, Cheetah," Catwoman said. "See? We're already working like a team."

"Great," Cheetah replied. "Now, partner, do you know where we can hide?"

"I have the *purrfect* place!" Catwoman replied.

Catwoman led Cheetah across the rooftops of Gotham City. Above them, a police helicopter used a bright searchlight to look for the gallery thief. But Catwoman knew every shadowy shelter. Soon, they were in a section of the city without lights. It was all shadows, but Cheetah sensed other things.

"What's that smell?" Cheetah asked, halting in her tracks. "Is that rotten fish?"

"Don't stop now! We're almost there!" Catwoman said.

"Where?" asked Cheetah. "The Gotham garbage dump?"

Catwoman led her partner into a dark warehouse. The wooden floors creaked. It sounded dangerous to Cheetah's ears. She could hear sloshing water.

"Welcome to my secret lair," replied Catwoman.

"This is your idea of a hideout?" Cheetah asked, holding her nose.

"Just wait and see," Catwoman said.

Cheetah followed Catwoman through a secret door. On the other side there was a beautiful room. The air smelled fresh, and the floors were covered with velvety carpet.

Catwoman stretched out in a big soft chair. "How do you like my hideout now?" she asked.

Cheetah laid down on a plump couch. "I could get used to this," she replied.

The cat burglars would not have been so relaxed if they knew that Batman was already at the art gallery. Two cat crimes in one night could mean only one thing to him: Catwoman was on the prowl!

*   *   *

Batman studied the crime scene. All clues pointed to Catwoman, except for the shredded costume on the floor. He took a microscope from his Utility Belt. He zoomed in on the display where the statue had stood. He was looking for fingerprints, but he found something unexpected.

The Dark Knight pulled a pair of tweezers from the Utility Belt. Then he carefully plucked a tiny hair from the display and held it up to the microscope.

"Interesting," said the super hero.

It wasn't human hair, but it wasn't animal hair, either. It was a combination of both. Batman knew that he had trouble on his hands. This cat crime was committed by a cat, all right, but not by Catwoman. Another cat crook was on the loose!

"Batman," a voice said from behind him. "I see you are on the trail of injustice."

"It's a road with no detour," Batman replied.

The Dark Knight turned and saw a tall woman dressed in bright red and blue. At her hip hung a glowing Golden Lasso.

"Hello, Wonder Woman," he said.

"Hello, my friend," replied the Amazon Princess. "I came to Gotham to help open an exhibit of Greek art at this gallery. May I offer my assistance?"

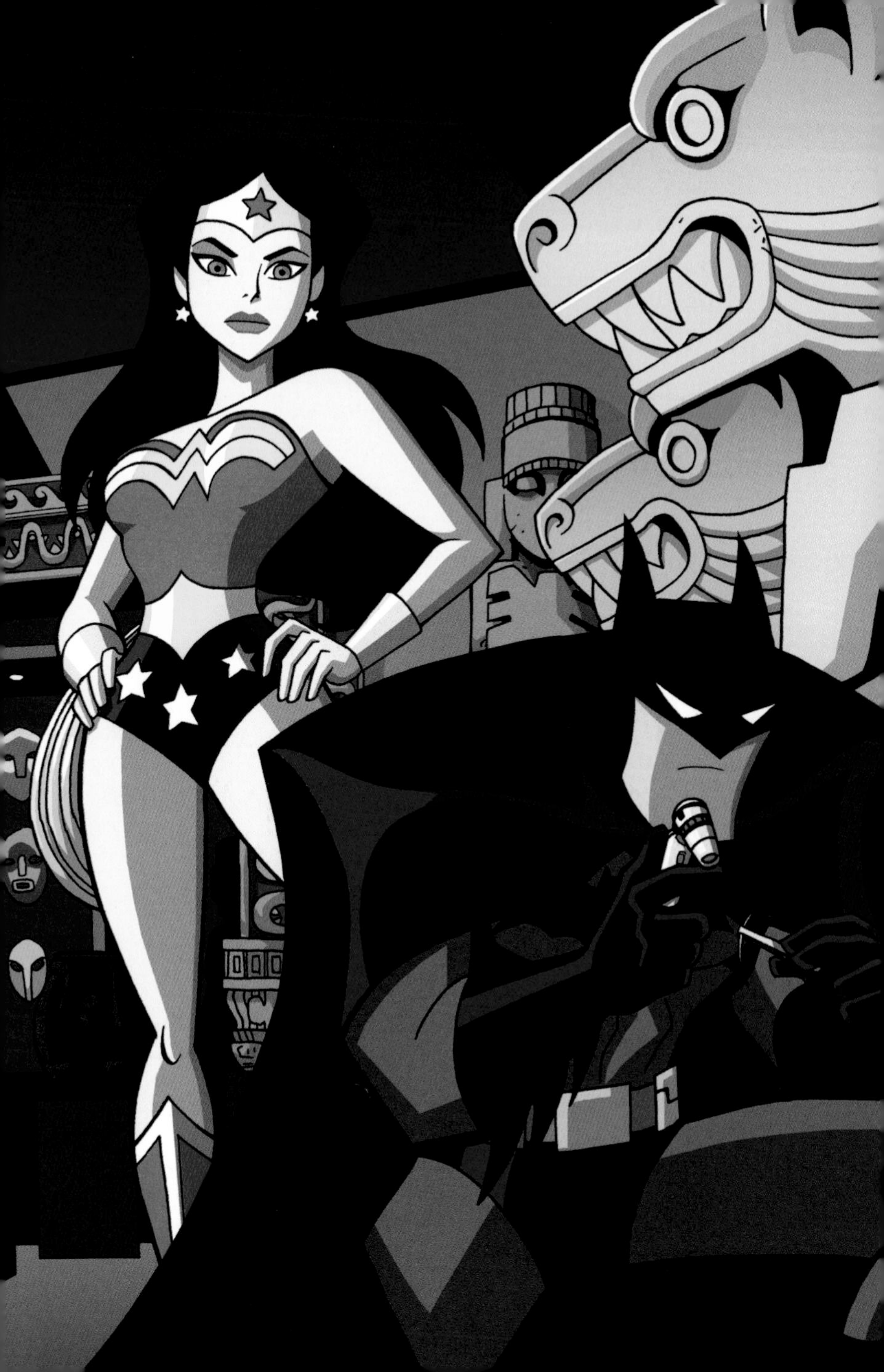

"Yes," Batman agreed. "Take a look at this and tell me what you think."

Batman handed Wonder Woman the hair sample. She did not need the microscope. Her eyesight alone was sharp enough.

"It looks like Gotham has a Cheetah on the loose," Wonder Woman said.

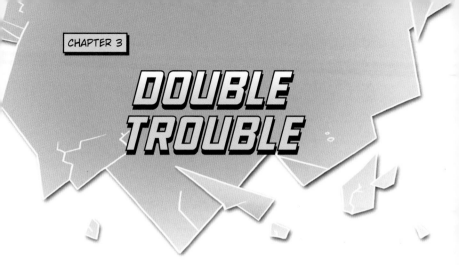

CHAPTER 3

DOUBLE TROUBLE

The next night, Cheetah slipped into the Caturanghua embassy as quiet as a cat. Her goal was to steal that country's jeweled crown, which was made in the shape of a running cheetah!

Cheetah sniffed the air, but she didn't smell any guards. That didn't mean there weren't other things protecting her chosen prey. Cheetah looked around the dark room. Her natural night vision detected a small blinking light. Then she saw three more in each corner of the room.

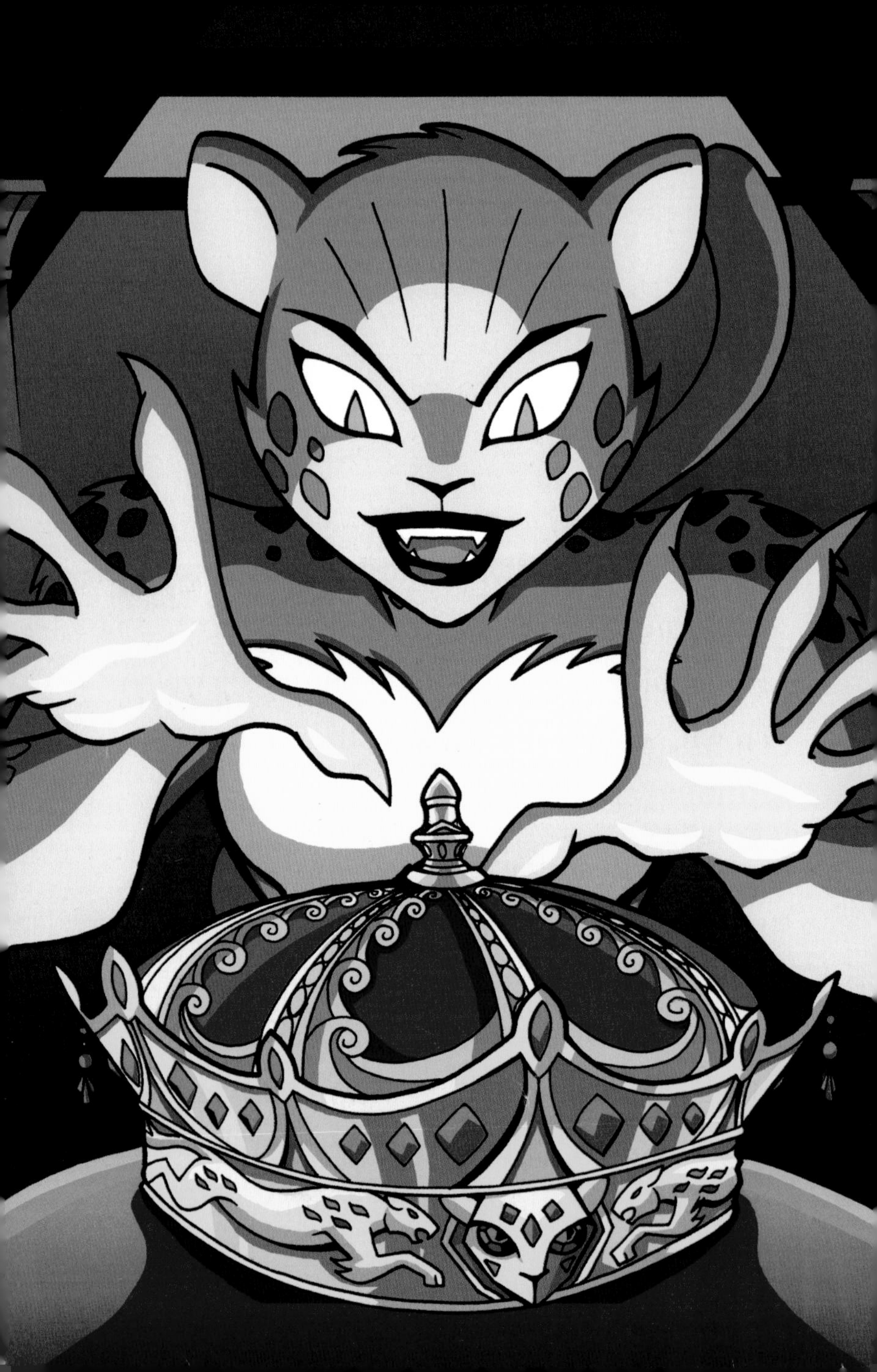

"HA! An alarm," Cheetah said. "Like that's going to stop me."

Cheetah crept on all fours to the control panel. She used one sharp claw to pop the cover, and another to cut a central wire. Suddenly, the blinking lights went dark.

Even so, Cheetah hesitated before opening the display case. She looked twice at the dead alarm panel just to make sure. Then she laughed at her fears and grabbed the crown from the case.

"Easy pickings," Cheetah said.

Cheetah slipped out of the embassy as quietly as she had entered it.

On the other side of the city, Catwoman crept through the shadows inside the Gotham History Museum. She made her way to the Egyptian section.

Spooky statues of dead pharaohs stared down at her. Then suddenly, a gleam of gold caught her attention. It came from a small coffin in the shape of a feline. Priceless gems covered the golden casket.

Catwoman knew she had found her prize — the mummy of Queen Cleopatra's cat. "Hello, kitty," she whispered. "You're coming home with me."

Catwoman unclipped a small tube from her belt. She gave it a slight squeeze. **PHWOOT!** White powder sprayed into the air. Red laser beams were suddenly revealed. They formed a security cage around the cat mummy's coffin.

The crafty cat took off her belt and flipped it inside out. Tiny mirrors were attached inside. Catwoman arranged them to reflect the lasers back on themselves.

"Here kitty kitty," she said, reaching in and removing the precious artifact.

Then Catwoman scampered away with her plunder.

*   *   *

Moments later, Batman was at the history museum investigating the theft. It was obvious how the crime had been committed. The mirrors were still in place, the lasers were still being reflected, and the powder tube was on the floor.

"This has all the earmarks of a cat burglar," he said. "Catwoman was here."

"Batman," Wonder Woman said over a communications link. "I am at the Caturanghua embassy. Their royal crown has been stolen. I have a witness who says he saw a giant cat enter the building."

"That crown is in the shape of a cheetah," Batman said. "That makes two cat crimes tonight, just like last night. Catwoman has been very busy."

"Catwoman?" Wonder Woman asked. "The evidence at the embassy points to Cheetah."

"Then it's a copycat crime," Batman concluded.

"Then we double our efforts to capture them," Wonder Woman said. "It is a good thing there are two of us on the case."

*   *   *

Across town, the comrades-in-crime relaxed in their hideout. Cheetah threw a handful of dollar bills into the air. They floated like confetti in a parade. She batted at the bills like a playful kitten.

"I came to Gotham to get some money, and now I have it!" Cheetah said, laughing.

"Not bad for two nights of work," Catwoman said. "If you call that work!"

Catwoman scrolled down some listings on a laptop. Cheetah stopped playing with her money and went over to see what her partner was doing.

"What are you looking for?" Cheetah asked.

"Our next target," Catwoman answered. "And a ride."

Cheetah smiled. She was starting to like these wild adventures. Catwoman knew how to make crime interesting!

"Found it," Catwoman said. "You're going to love this."

CHAPTER 4

CATCH ME IF YOU CAN

A little while later, the cat crooks crouched on the roof of a car dealership. Cheetah used her claws to cut through the skylight. They dropped down into the showroom. No alarms went off.

Cheetah went straight to a sleek and shiny convertible. She ran her hands over the hood as if stroking a pet. "I like your idea of a 'ride,' my friend," Cheetah said.

"It's only fitting," Catwoman replied. "We're the cats of crime. We should ride in a car that's as sleek as a cat, too."

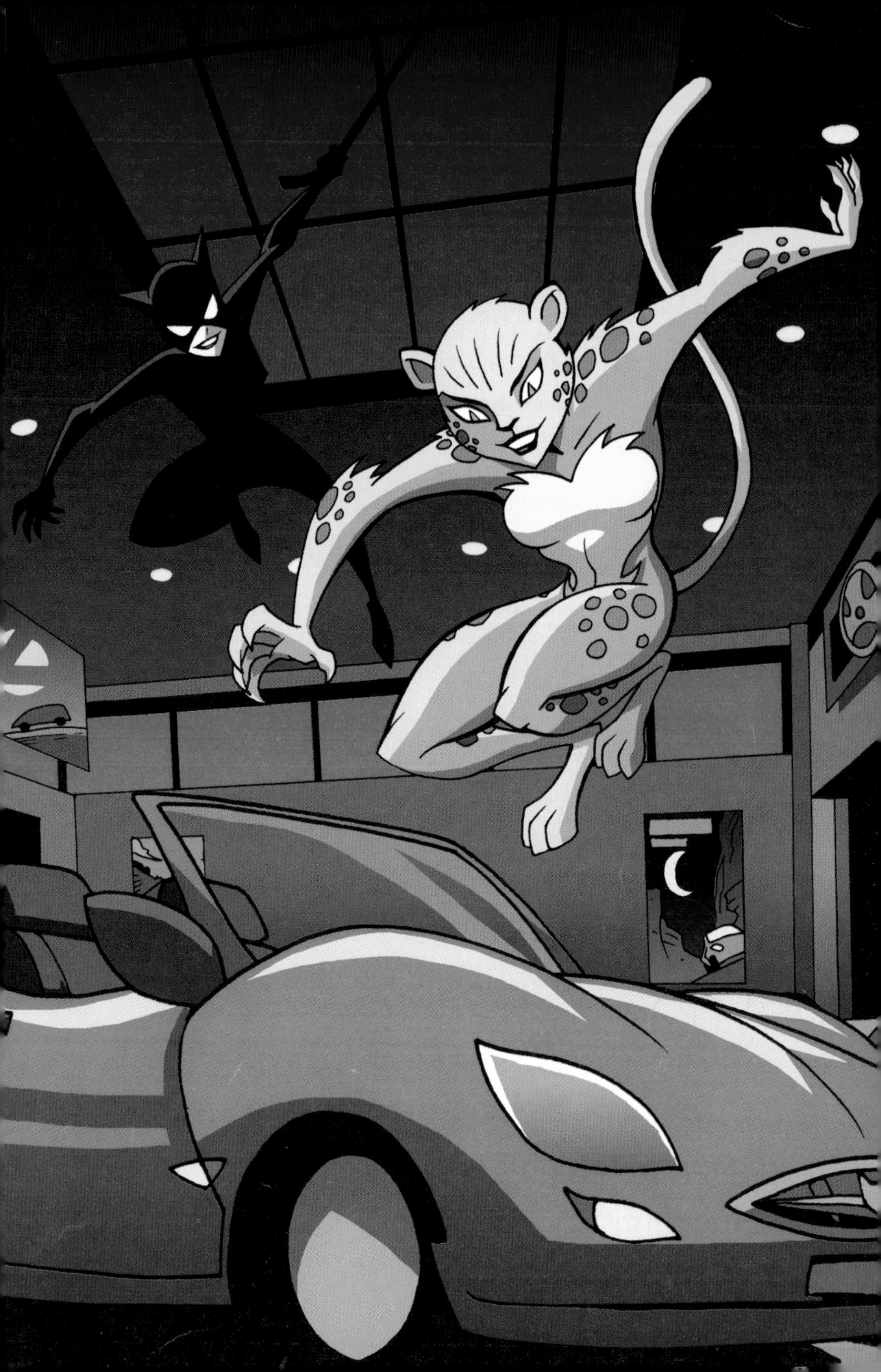

"It's *purrfect*," Cheetah said with a grin. She jumped into the driver's seat.

"I want to drive!" shouted Catwoman.

"You can drive on the getaway," Cheetah said.

That appealed to Catwoman. She got into the car. Cheetah turned the key and stepped on the gas. The tires squealed as the car zoomed forward.

CRASH!! The super-villain drove the car right through the display window!

The car skidded and swerved as it hit the streets of Gotham. Catwoman didn't know if she should be afraid or excited. Cheetah was a wild driver.

"This is better than running over rooftops," Cheetah said. "My feet get tired doing that."

It didn't take them long to reach their destination. Cheetah brought the car to a screeching halt in front of the Asia Club. Inside the club was a collection of rare katana swords.

The two villains didn't hesitate this time. They smashed through the front door, and let the alarms go off. They were in and out of the club with their prize in no time at all. Catwoman jumped into the driver's seat of the car. Cheetah landed in the passenger seat with her arms full of valuable katana swords.

ZOOOM! Suddenly, a large black car sped around the corner. It was the Batmobile! Cheetah and Catwoman looked at each other. Instead of being worried, they started to laugh.

"It's time for the chase!" Cheetah said.

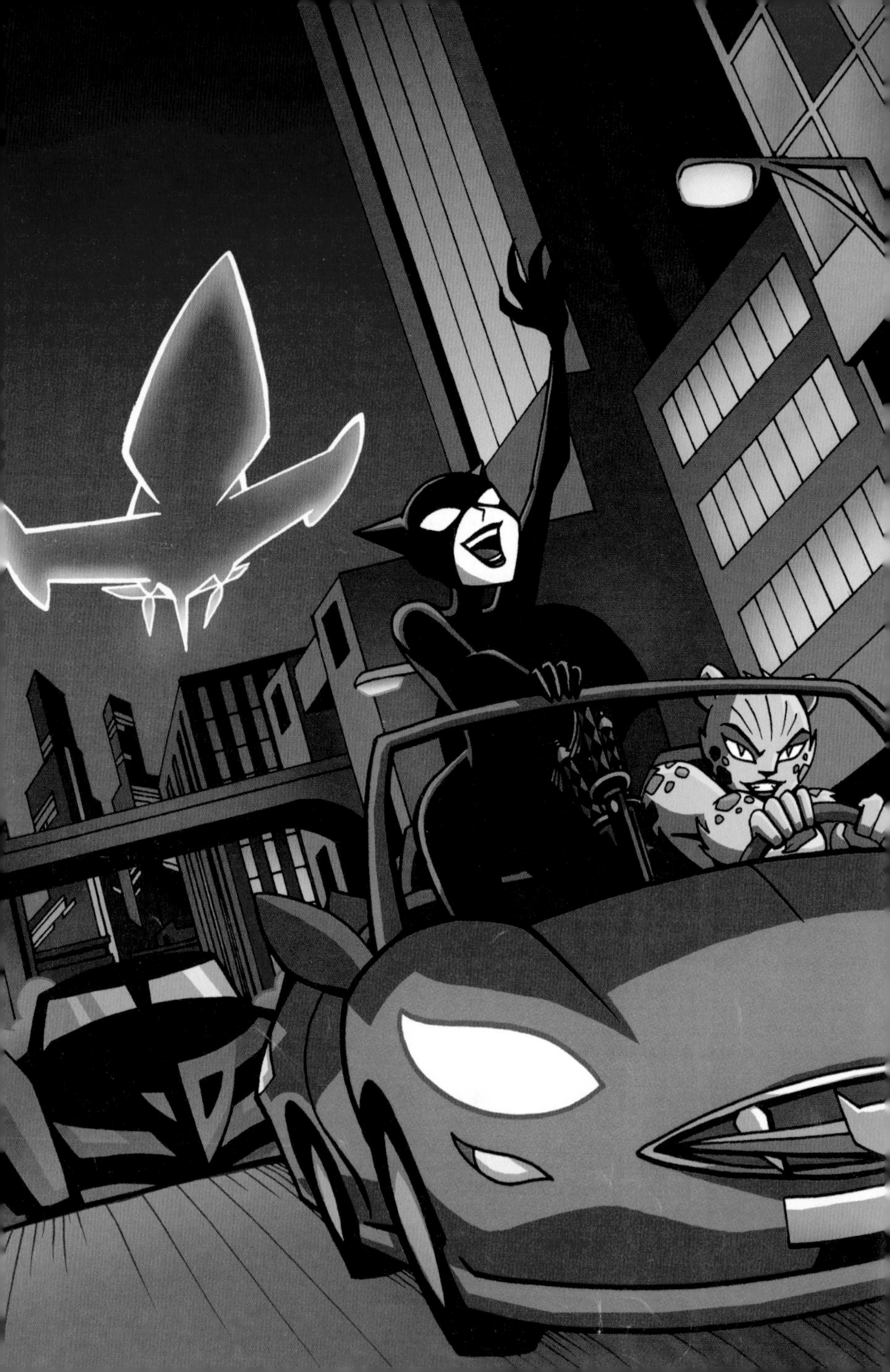

"Now we can have some real fun!" Catwoman said.

VROOOOOM! The sports car took off down the street at top speed, and the Batmobile followed. The two cars zigged and zagged along the dark streets of nighttime Gotham City.

"Batman to Wonder Woman," the Dark Knight said over the communications link. "Do you have our quarry in sight?"

"Yes," she replied. "I'm right above them."

Wonder Woman flew in her Invisible Jet. She would be able to follow the feline felons from the air if they got away from Batman. "They're heading for a bridge," the Amazon Princess told her partner. "I can use my jet to block the road there."

"Good idea," Batman replied. "And I'll block their exit."

Cheetah and Catwoman were having a grand time leading Batman on a wild chase. They were laughing so hard they had tears in their eyes. Ahead of them was Gotham Bridge. Cheetah had to blink a few times before she could focus her sharp eye on that strange sight in front of them. She saw Wonder Woman, but the Amazon seemed to be sitting in midair.

"The plane!" Cheetah realized. "Her Invisible Jet!"

There was no time for Cheetah to explain to Catwoman. They had only a few seconds before the car crashed into the Invisible Jet. Cheetah grabbed the steering wheel and turned it. SKKKREEEEEEE

The convertible veered off the road.
It crashed through the guardrail and
went sailing over the river. Cheetah and
Catwoman weren't wearing seat belts. They
suddenly found themselves flying through
the air. Their laughter turned to screams.

"Heeeellllp!" they yelled.

At that moment, a Golden Lasso
wrapped around Cheetah, and a black rope
snagged Catwoman. **SPRONGG!**

The crooks immediately stopped falling.
Above them, Wonder Woman stood on
the edge of the bridge. She had Cheetah
hanging by her Golden Lasso. Standing
next to her, Batman had Catwoman
dangling at the end of the Batrope.

"Your cat crime spree is finished,"
Batman said.

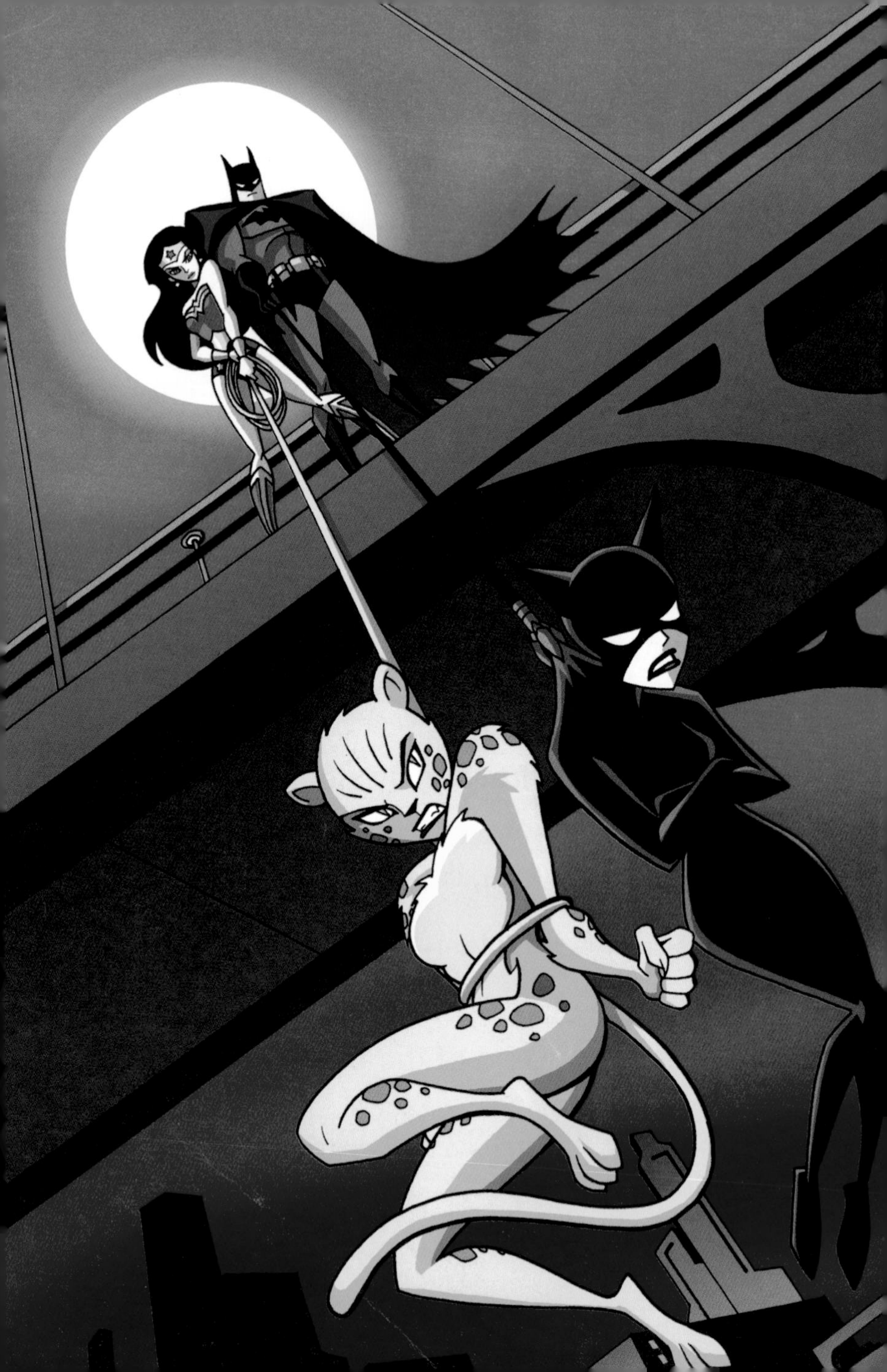

Neither of the crooks moved as they were set down on the ground. They sat on the pavement as if their legs couldn't hold them upright. They looked humbled and defeated, but it was all an act.

Suddenly, Catwoman sliced through the Batrope with her steel claws. She used her acrobatic skills to knock Batman into Wonder Woman. When the surprised Amazon Princess let go of the magic lasso, Catwoman was able to untie Cheetah from its coils. The feline felons were free!

"Split up!" Cheetah said.

The villains ran in opposite directions.

"I'll go after Cheetah!" Wonder Woman shouted.

"And I'll get Catwoman," Batman replied. "Be careful, they're crafty!"

CHAPTER 5

CAT TRAP

Cheetah was very fast, and so was Wonder Woman. But Cheetah did not keep the race on level ground. She used her catlike agility to jump and swing over everything in her way.

Cheetah was trying to make Wonder Woman trip or crash into something. And while there were many close calls, Wonder Woman stayed on Cheetah's tail.

I need Wonder Woman to chase something else, Cheetah thought. *I know just the thing.*

Although Cheetah didn't know Gotham City very well, she knew it had a zoo. She also knew it was nearby because she could smell the scent of lions and tigers in the air.

"I need a little help from my feline friends," Cheetah said.

She raced into the zoo, just barely ahead of Wonder Woman. The Amazon was fast! So was Cheetah, but she could only run at high speed for a short burst of time. She was already slowing down. She headed for the lion cages.

"Wake up, my cat cousins!" Cheetah snarled as she ripped open the metal cage.

All the predators woke up. They roared at the sight of freedom. Cheetah laughed as Wonder Woman stopped chasing her and rushed to round up the big cats.

When Cheetah returned to the secret lair, she was worn out. That last run had been exhausting. She was tired and sweaty, and she had lost the katana swords. Those were worth money!

If that wasn't bad enough now, Batman and Wonder Woman were after her.

"This town is getting dangerous," Cheetah said. "I'm leaving."

"What? You're not going to say goodbye to your partner?" a voice said.

Catwoman entered the secret lair and stepped into the light. "I didn't know if you were coming back," she said.

"Neither did I," Cheetah admitted.

"Well, as long as you're here," said Catwoman, "maybe you'd like to stick around for one last cat crime."

* * *

Meanwhile, Wonder Woman and Batman reviewed video of the last heist from inside their vehicles. The Batmobile and Invisible Jet had digitally recorded the entire event.

"They've teamed up," Batman said.

"But Cheetah usually works alone," Wonder Woman replied over the radio.

"So does Catwoman," added Batman.

"Then why are they working together this time around?" Wonder Woman asked.

"They must be planning something neither of them can do alone," Batman said. "Something big."

"Something to do with cats," Wonder Woman said.

Batman accessed the Batmobile's computer. Wonder Woman linked into the information components of her Amazonian jet. The duo searched for clues to where the cat criminals would strike next.

"Nothing," Wonder Woman said.

"Then let's make something," Batman said. "We can lure them into a trap."

"Do you remember the story of the Trojan Horse?" Wonder Woman said.

"Are you suggesting that we hide inside a giant wooden cat?" Batman replied.

Wonder Woman let out a laugh and then held up her Golden Lasso. She stretched the glittering rope and dangled it like a piece of yarn.

"Not a *cat*," she said mysteriously.

* * *

The next night, Cheetah and Catwoman were on the prowl again. They wanted to make up for the loss of the katana swords. Their target was a fantastic golden ball of string. It was on display at the same art gallery where Cheetah had stolen the jaguar statue. Sneaking in was easy.

"No one would think we'd come here twice," Cheetah whispered to her partner.

"The fools didn't even bother to change the security system," Catwoman observed.

They stood next to the giant gleaming ball of golden string. It looked like a huge cat toy.

"How are we going to get this out of here?" Cheetah wondered.

"It's simple," Catwoman said, laughing. "We roll it!"

The kitty crooks both shoved the giant ball. The string started to unravel. It twisted in the air as if it were alive! Then the shining strands wrapped around Cheetah and Catwoman.

The golden string tightened around the comrades-in-crime. They could not move. Catwoman tried cutting the string with her steel claws. So did Cheetah. Nothing worked. Helplessly, they struggled against their capture.

"You will not resist," a voice told them.

Suddenly, Cheetah and Catwoman felt their bodies go limp. They couldn't help it. They had to obey the voice.

The ball of string continued to unravel.

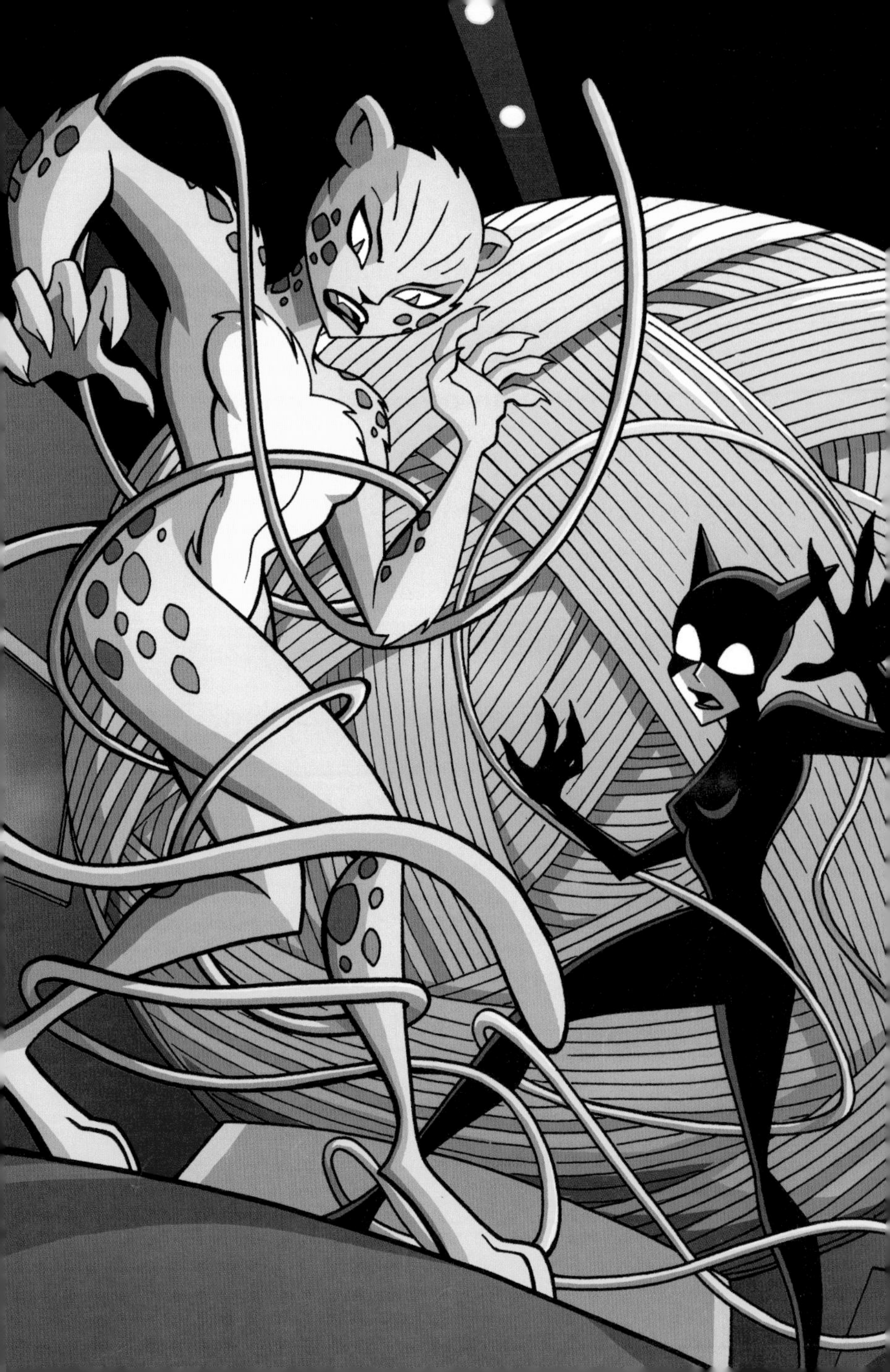

As the ball grew smaller and smaller, there stood Batman and Wonder Woman. The princess held the end of the golden string in her hands.

"Oh, no," Cheetah moaned. "That wasn't a ball of gold, it was Wonder Woman's Golden Lasso!"

"They were hiding inside it all this time," Catwoman said. "We were tricked!"

"The Greeks tricked the Trojans with a wooden horse," Wonder Woman said.

"And an Amazon Princess tricked two cats with a magic string," Batman said.

"I really wanted that ball of gold," Catwoman pouted.

"Next time, my friend," Cheetah said with a wicked smile. "This cat won't stay caged for long."

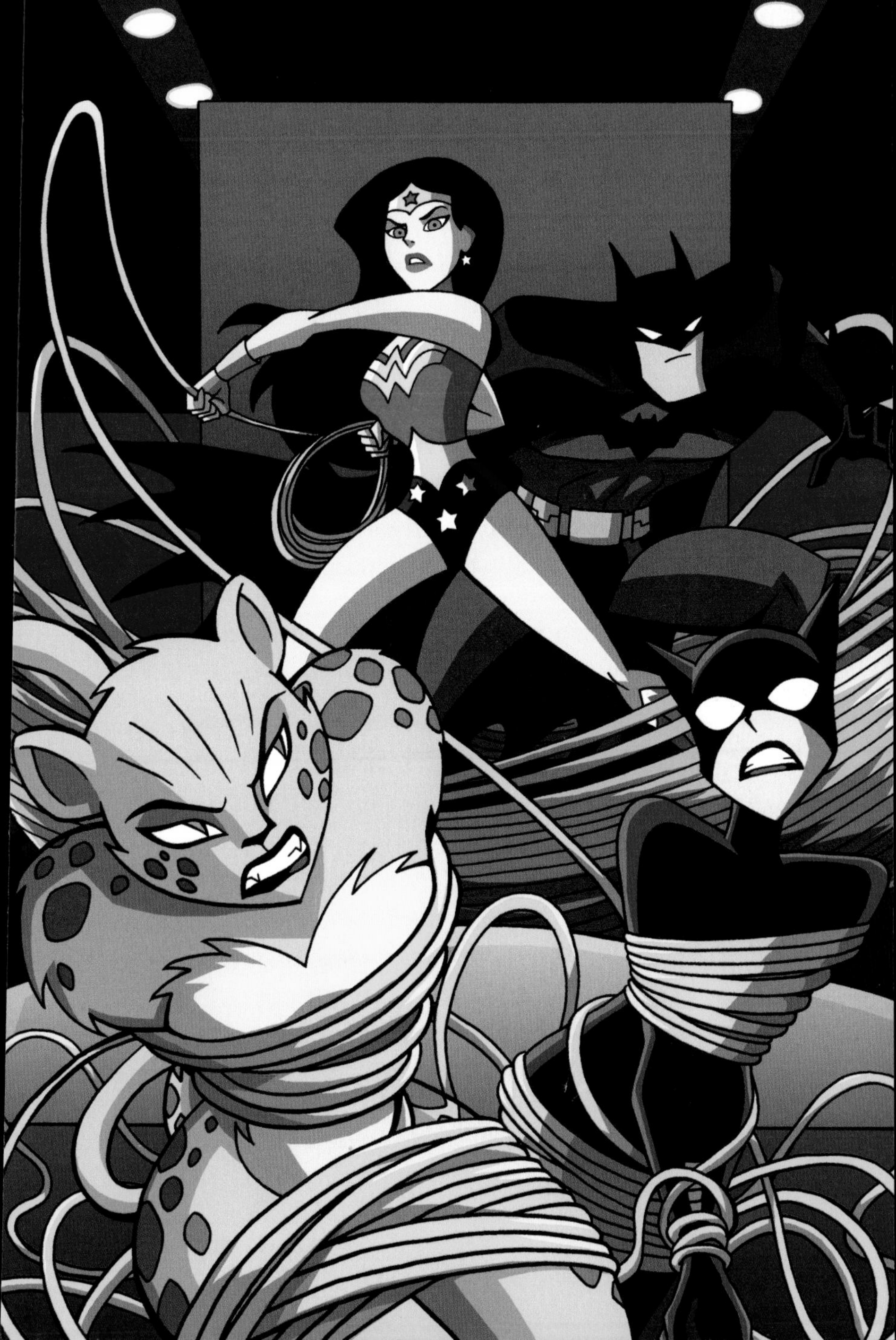

BIOGRAPHIES

Laurie S. Sutton has read comics since she was a kid. She grew up to become an editor for Marvel, DC Comics, Starblaze, and Tekno Comics. She has written *Adam Strange* for DC, *Star Trek: Voyager* for Marvel, plus *Star Trek: Deep Space Nine* and *Witch Hunter* for Malibu Comics. There are long boxes of comics in her closet where there should be clothing and shoes. Laurie has lived all over the world, and currently resides in Florida.

Luciano Vecchio was born in 1982 and currently lives in Buenos Aires, Argentina. With experience in illustration, animation and comics, his works have been published in the US, Spain, UK, France, and Argentina. Credits include Ben 10 (DC Comics), Cruel Thing (Norma), Unseen Tribe (Zuda Comics), and Sentinels (Drumfish Productions).

GLOSSARY

acrobatics (ak-ruh-BAT-iks)—difficult gymnastic acts that are often performed in the air

cautiously (KAW-shuhss-lee)—if you do something cautiously, you try hard to avoid mistakes or danger

detour (DEE-tour)—a longer alternative route usually taken when the direct route is closed

felines (FEE-linez)—cats or having to do with cats

imitating (IM-uh-tate-ing)—copying or mimicking someone or something

katana (kuh-TAH-nuh)—a long, curved sword traditionally used by Japanese samurai

predators (PRED-uh-turz)—animals that hunt other animals for food

prowl (PROUL)—move around quietly and secretly like a cat stalking its prey

unravel (uhn-RAV-uhl)—to unwind a tangled mass of string, or to search for and discover the truth about a complex situation

withdrawal (with-DRAW-uhl)—if you make a withdrawal, you take money out of the bank

DISCUSSION QUESTIONS

1. Who was more to blame for the cat crimes — Cheetah or Catwoman? Why?

2. Wonder Woman uses her Golden Lasso to trick Catwoman and Cheetah. Is tricking someone ever okay? Discuss your answers.

3. This book has ten illustrations. Which one is your favorite? Why?

WRITING PROMPTS

1. If you could have any of the superpowers used in this book by any character, which superpower would you want? Write about it.

2. Cheetah and Catwoman stole a series of cat-related valuables. What are some other cat-like treasures that the two feline criminals might have stolen if they hadn't gotten caught?

3. Batman and Wonder Woman team up to take down Catwoman and Cheetah's partnership. Create your own super hero or super-villain partner. What does he or she look like? What are his or her powers? Write about your sidekick, then draw a picture of the two of you together.

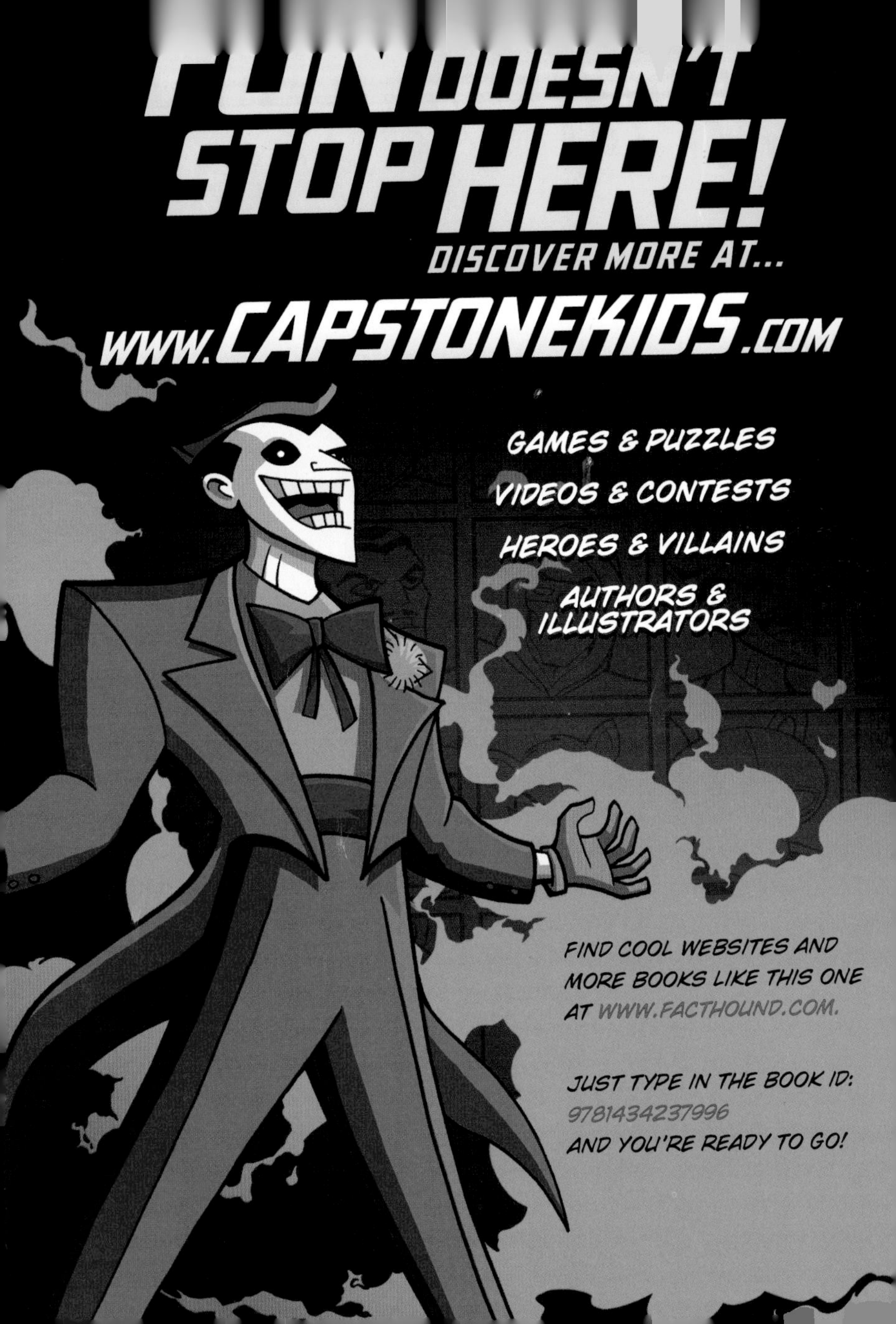
FUN DOESN'T STOP HERE!
DISCOVER MORE AT...
WWW.CAPSTONEKIDS.COM
GAMES & PUZZLES
VIDEOS & CONTESTS
HEROES & VILLAINS
AUTHORS & ILLUSTRATORS
FIND COOL WEBSITES AND MORE BOOKS LIKE THIS ONE AT WWW.FACTHOUND.COM.
JUST TYPE IN THE BOOK ID: 9781434237996 AND YOU'RE READY TO GO!

LOOK FOR MORE

SUPER DC HEROES VILLAINS

SUPER DC HEROES VILLAINS
BRIGHT · VECCHIO
LEX LUTHOR
AND THE
KRYPTONITE CAVERNS

LEX LUTHOR AND THE KRYPTONITE CAVERNS

SUPER DC HEROES VILLAINS
SINESTRO
AND THE RING OF FEAR
SUTTON
McMANUS
LOUGHRIDGE

SINESTRO AND THE RING OF FEAR

SUPER DC HEROES VILLAINS
JOKER
ON THE
HIGH SEAS
BRIGHT
McMANUS
LOUGHRIDGE

JOKER ON THE HIGH SEAS

SUPER DC HEROES VILLAINS
BLACK MANTA
AND THE
OCTOPUS ARMY
MASON
VECCHIO

BLACK MANTA AND THE OCTOPUS ARMY

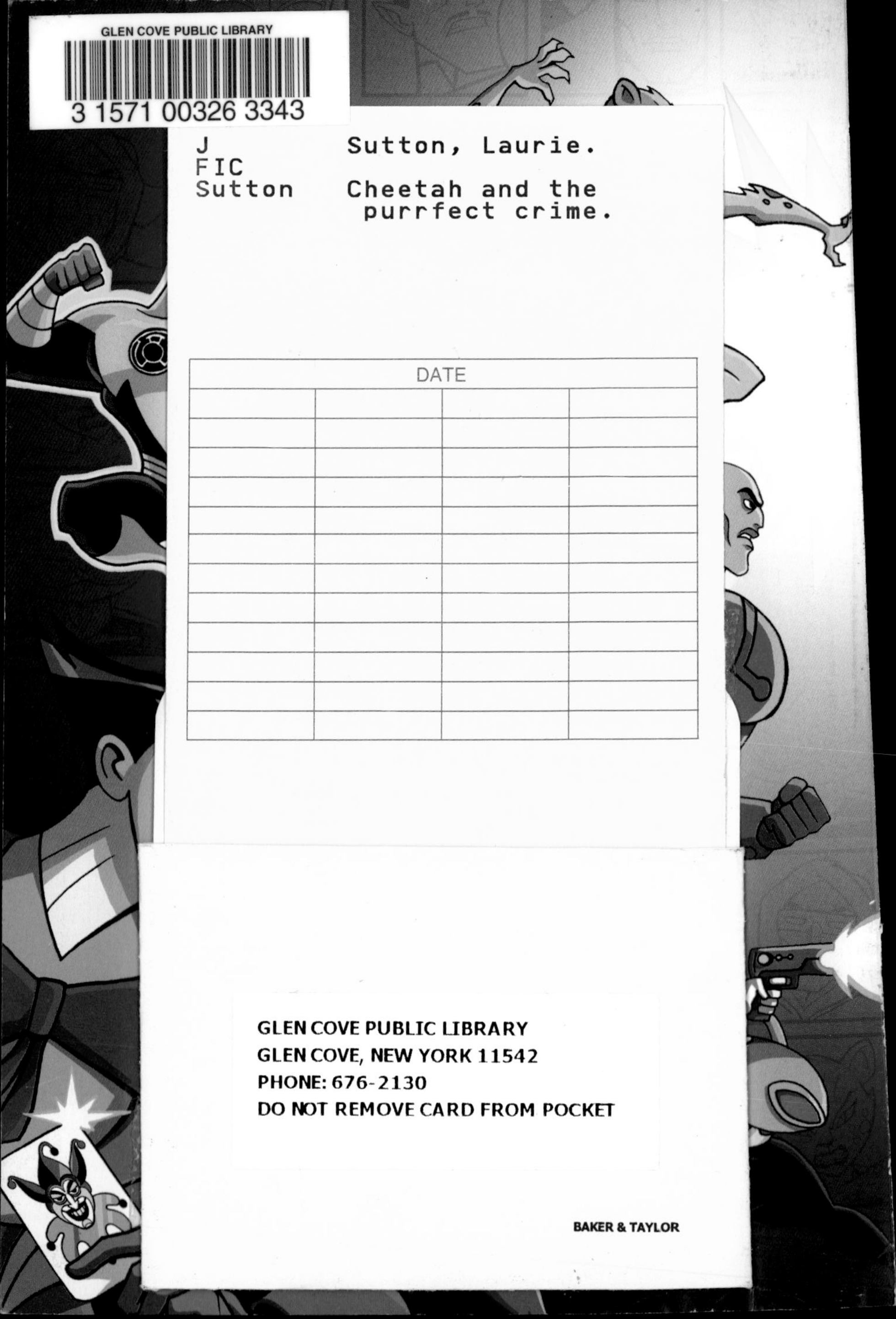